THE DAYS OF THE PHARAOHS

Living In Another Time

THE DAYS OF THE PHARAOHS

Illustrations by Ginette Hoffmann
Text by Michel Sethus
Translated by Christopher Sharp

Silver Burdett Company
Morristown, New Jersey and Agincourt, Ontario

For my parents,
Ginette Hoffmann

Series coordinated by Michel Pierre
in collaboration with Elisabeth Sebaoun

English text consultant:
Donald R. Laing, Jr.,
Associate Professor of Classics,
Case Western Reserve University

Library of Congress Cataloging-in-Publication Data

Sethus, Michel.
    The days of the pharaohs.

    (Living in another time)
    Translation of: A l'epoque des pharaons.
    Summary: Presents a glimpse of life in ancient
Egypt by following the daily activities of a family.
    [1. Egypt—Civilization—To 332 B.C.—Fiction]
I. Hoffmann, Ginette, ill. II. Title. III. Series:
Des enfants dans l'histoire. English.
PZ7.S498Day   1986   86-6764
ISBN 0-382-09177-9

Published pursuant to an agreement with Casterman, Paris
First published in French by Casterman as *Des enfants dans
l'Histoire: A L'epoque des Pharaons*

First published in the United States in 1986
by Silver Burdett Company
Morristown, New Jersey

Published simultaneously in Canada
by GLC/Silver Burdett Publishers

Table of Contents

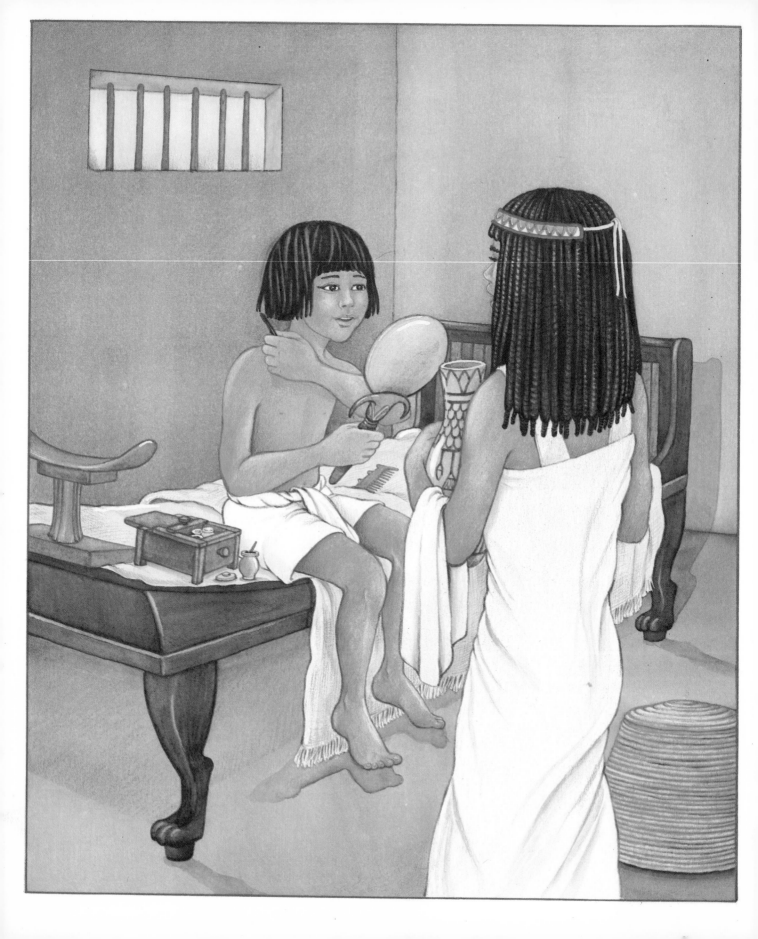

Living in the City

The first signs of daylight appeared on the horizon. The city of Thebes was about to begin a new day. Hundreds of sun-dried brick houses and gigantic temples were slowly shaking off Nut's (the goddess of the sky) starry blanket. The Nile shimmered in the early morning light. Suddenly the sun's rays grew brighter. Light rushed through the streets, waking households and breaking the quiet of the night. It was the first hour of the day, or what the Egyptians called "brightness."

Sethi's room was suddenly flooded with light. He opened his eyes only to close them again. The sun was too strong. His bed was made of wood and had legs carved in the shape of lions' paws. A linen sheet covered his bed, and a wooden headrest served as a pillow.

"Can you hear the sparrows chirping? They have no trouble getting up to welcome the new day! Get out of your bed, lazy bones," Madja, the nursemaid, said as she walked into the room. She was carrying a pitcher of water and a washbowl. Sethi washed himself carefully, and then wrapped a white linen loincloth around his waist.

7

"You're proud of your new loincloth, aren't you! Not so long ago you weren't wearing anything, like your younger sisters!" Madja said, teasing him.

"That's not true! My father's let me wear a loincloth for almost a year now."

Sethi looked at himself in the shiny bronze mirror his nursemaid handed him. He was nine years old, with brown-colored skin and neatly cut hair that surrounded his cheerful face and twinkling dark eyes.

As soon as he was ready, Sethi left his bedroom and ran down the wooden stairs to the ground floor of the house. The young boy met his mother, Nefert. She was giving orders to the servants.

"Nekhti, take these bags of grain up to the roof, away from the mice. And you, Hori, don't forget to bake the bread and make the beer."

The bread and beer were prepared at the same time. This was because beer was made by crumbling up lightly baked bread in a liquid made from dates. The mixture was brewed and filtered, and then it sat and slowly fermented. Finally, it was poured into earthenware jars and sealed with clay tops.

"You're baking so much bread today," Sethi said to his mother.

"Your brains aren't any bigger than a frog's!" Nefert answered with a smile. "Have you forgotten that today your father is having a big banquet for all those who worked with him?"

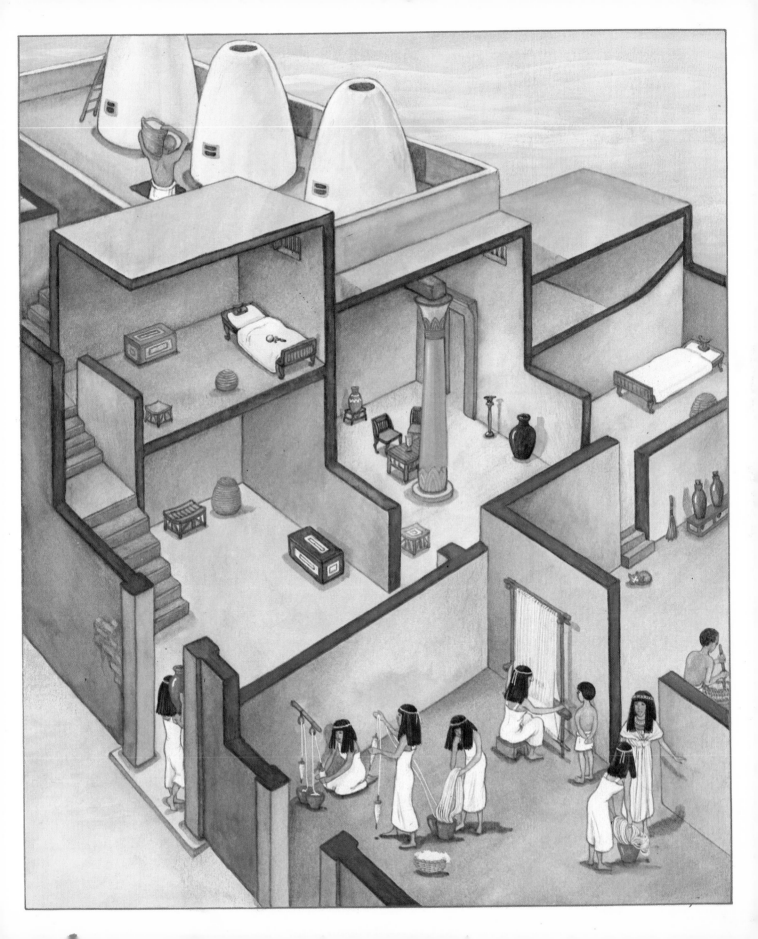

In a corner of the hall, servants were making linen cloth. It would be used to make clothes for the whole family. The linen thread was spun on a bobbin and strung up on a vertical two-bar loom. The loom was made of two forked branches set in the ground and joined by two wooden horizontal bars, or *crosspieces*. Lengthwise threads, or *warp*, were stretched between these two bars. Linen crosswise threads, or *weft*, were woven through the warp threads and flattened with a wooden bar. This was repeated until the loom was filled.

As he nibbled on a honey cookie, Sethi admired the swift movements of the weaver. All of a sudden a hand came to rest on his shoulder. It was Rekhmire, his father, and beside him were two little girls. They were Sethi's little sisters. All they wore were blue stone necklaces.

"It's time to go, my son, or you will be late for school at the House of Life. Your teacher will not be pleased with you."

"I'm on my way, Father!"

The boy picked up his writing materials and a few potsherds (pieces of broken pottery) on which to write his exercises.

After saying goodbye to his parents, Sethi left the house. In the garden his dog greeted him. It jumped all over him and barked with joy.

Preparing the dough

The dough is placed in red-hot molds.

Different forms of Egyptian bread

The fermented liquid is poured into earthenware jars.

Lightly baked bread is made into crumbs and mixed with a liquid made from dates.

Food in the Days of the Pharaohs

In ancient Egypt most people ate bread, onions, and fish (either fried or dried). Only the nobles, priests, scribes, and rich shopkeepers could afford to eat meat—on special occasions. Poultry (geese, pigeons, and ducks) was in plentiful supply. Mutton and beef were reserved for banquets and feasts. Because meat did not keep well in the hot Egyptian climate, it was eaten as soon as the animal was killed.

Beer was a popular drink, along with wine. Dates and figs were the most common types of fruit, but there were also pomegranates, grapes, melons, and watermelons.

The Funeral Procession

Sethi's dog followed him as he crossed the garden. He went to the pond surrounded by willow and locust trees. The young boy stopped and admired the lotus flowers that seemed to float on the water. The day before, Nefert had told him about the legend of the lotus. The lotus had come out of the water and given birth to the sun in the world's first morning, when the universe was created.

Kheti, the gardener, was busy taking water from the pond with a *shadoof.* This was a long pole that moved on tall posts planted in the ground. A water skin was attached with a rope to one end of the pole. The other end was packed with mud to act as a counterbalance weight.

"May I try?" the boy asked. Sethi pulled on the rope to lower the water skin into the pond. Thanks to the weight on the other end of the pole, the water skin came back up filled with water.

"This saves us lots of hard work. Even you can use it!" the gardener exclaimed, laughing.

"But you have to have muscles," Sethi replied, proud of what he could do.

13

Sethi left the peaceful garden and came out on a street. Dusty and full of noise, it was lined with stands of all kinds. At one stand there were onions and at another, soap. At a third stand a man was making a pair of leather sandals, and at yet another, a fisherman was selling dried fish. A little farther down the street, there was a man with two tame monkeys, who were making funny faces. Sethi looked around. He recognized old Ahmose, the fruit seller, and went to say hello. Hardly a day went by when Ahmose wasn't at the market. He knew much about the world, because he was very old. Sethi liked to talk with him.

"Stay and talk with me for awhile," the old man said. "You can't get by now anyway, look!"

A funeral procession blocked the street as it moved on its way toward the river pier. A richly decorated coffin was carried along on a sledge pulled by men. Priests sprinkled it with water to purify it. Mourners, with mud-covered faces, sobbed and moaned.

Ahmose shook his head. "Such is the fate of all men, rich or poor! But there's nothing to be afraid of, young lad. Life continues on after death. The burial only changes the place where you live. That is why it is so important to make mummies out of the dead, so that their bodies are preserved. In any case, this one will have a comfortable tomb, judging from the things the servants are carrying."

The procession slowly passed by. Some of the men carried clothes, sandals, and jewelry boxes. There were chairs, stools, a bed—enough furniture to fill a house!

Others carried jars filled with wine or baskets filled with bread, fruit, or poultry.

"Everyone hopes to find the same life when he dies," Ahmose said. "Everything you see here will be placed in the tomb. There will also be small statues called servant-statues. If the gods summon the dead person to do some hard tasks, these statues will serve and do the work for him. In that way, eternity will be pleasant for the person who is no longer living—provided that the judgment is favorable for him, of course."

"My father told me about that," Sethi exclaimed. "The dead person is brought before the great god Osiris and the other judges. His heart is weighed on a balance by Anubis, the jackal-headed god. Thoth, who has the head of an ibis (a bird), writes down the results on tablets. If the dead person's heart is heavy with evil deeds, he will not be able to have eternal happiness. But if his heart is as light as a feather, he will be welcomed by the gods."

Sethi left Ahmose, who praised the boy for his knowledge, and went down to the river. The body and all its possessions had been placed on a boat, which would cross the Nile. The burial grounds were on the opposite side of the river—on the west bank, where the sun set.

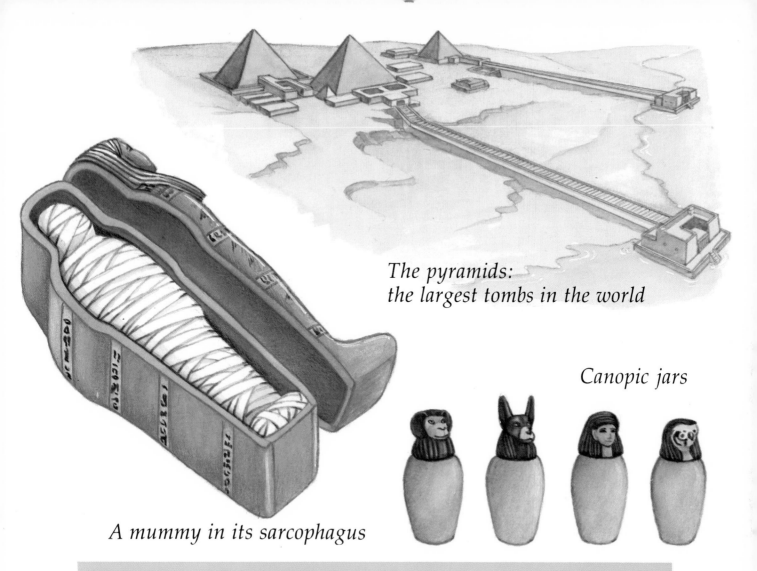

*The pyramids:
the largest tombs in the world*

Canopic jars

A mummy in its sarcophagus

Mummies and Tombs

Mummifying the dead was a job done by *embalmers*. After removing the brain, they took out all of the body's organs and placed them in four jars now called *canopic jars*. Then the embalmers covered the body for several weeks with salt, which slowly dried it. After that they wrapped the body in cloth bandages and placed *amulets* (good-luck charms) between the bandages to protect the deceased. Finally the body was put in a painted *sarcophagus* (coffin), and then placed in the tomb.

The tombs of wealthy people were richly decorated and furnished. The most sumptuous of them all were the tombs of the Egyptian *pharaohs* (rulers). Some were buried more than 5,000 years ago in huge stone monuments called *pyramids*.

Writing School

Sethi knew he was going to be late for school. He had stayed with his friend Ahmose much too long. He began to run, hoping he might still get there on time. When he got to the House of Life, where he studied, he was all out of breath. The building was a part of the temple of the god Amon. It was mainly used to teach future priests and transcribers of sacred texts. Sethi could have attended another school in Thebes. It was a school open only to sons of nobles and princes. But Rekhmire had preferred to send his son to the House of Life because the teacher, User, was his friend. User was a learned scribe. He spent much of his time reading, writing, and teaching.

User was already sitting on the floor cross-legged, and his pupils had formed a circle around him.

"Come in, Sethi," User said.

"Good morning, master," the child replied as he sat down next to his friend Tuti. Sethi quickly took out his writing tools. He had a writing palette with two inkpots. One contained red ink, the other black. In a small opening in the center of the writing palette, there were a couple of thin reed stems, which he used for writing. The end of the stem had to be chewed in order to obtain the right shape.

"Master, when will we be able to write on papyrus?" Tuti asked.

"First you must practice hard and get better," he answered. "Papyrus is very expensive and is only used for important texts."

"Why is it so expensive?" another child asked. "So much of it grows on the banks of the Nile."

"That may be true," User replied. "But although it is easy to pick, it is not easy to turn into sheets. First of all the plant must be as tall as two men before it can be cut. Then you have to remove the outer covering and cut the soft inner part into thin slices. After that the thin slices are placed on top of one another to form two layers. They are covered with a piece of cloth and then hammered to make a sheet of papyrus. To make a roll, a large number of these sheets are attached to one another.

"Do you think all this work is done so that you can have scrap sheets on which to practice your writing exercises? You have wooden tablets that you can cover with stucco (marble powder mixed with glue) as often as you like. You can also use potsherds. They don't cost anything. Be happy with what you have for now. Well, enough of this talk, let's get down to work!"

When he finished giving a lesson on counting, User taught the children how to write a text, using hieroglyphics. The pupils dipped their reeds in water and then in ink. Then they wrote titles in red and the rest of the text in black. Sethi, began practicing and carefully traced the complicated signs on his tablet.

Hieroglyphics were small drawings representing animals, objects, or human beings. They could be written in many different ways, horizontally or in columns, left to right, or right to left. It was difficult to write hieroglyphics, but if one worked very carefully, the result could be magnificent.

User looked at each boy's work and made some corrections. He praised Sethi's work, "If you keep working like that, someday you'll be a respected scribe. Your life will be one of pleasure and wealth. You will not have to be a soldier and fight far away from home, nor will you have your hands calloused and blistered like workers. You'll never go hungry and you will give orders to others. You'll be responsible for counting the sheep and cattle the peasants bring to the temple to pay their taxes. You will be the one to check and see that each person gives the right amount.

"If you're good at your job, you'll be rewarded, and you will become more powerful. The king may even place his trust in you. Perhaps he'll summon you to his side as he has done with your father, the surveyor, who helps build temples! I want all of you to know that he who can read and write will be a wealthy man, because the profession of scribe is worth more than any other."

Tuti leaned over to Sethi and whispered, "You're lucky our teacher thinks so highly of you. Yesterday he was so angry with me that he called me goose of the Nile. 'You're like that animal,' he shouted at me, 'you only bring trouble!'" Sethi could not help laughing at the idea of his friend being called a goose.

Hieroglyphics

The ancient Egyptians invented a beautiful form of writing, called *hieroglyphics*. To write correctly, one had to know how to use and combine over 700 pictures. It was very complicated because each hieroglyph could have several meanings.

Sometimes the symbol's meaning was very clear. For example, the hieroglyph ~ˣ meant a "viper with horns." If the viper crawled along a flat line ~ˣ the verb "to crawl" was meant. If it returned to its hole ~ˀ the verb "to enter" was written. If it left the hole ꭓ~ the verb "to go out" was indicated.

A hieroglyph could also represent a sound. The viper, for example, represented the *F* sound because the ancient Egyptian name for viper began with an *F*.

During this lesson, Sethi learned the following hieroglyphs.

An owl   or the *M* sound
Water   or the *N* sound
A mouth   or the *R* sound
Bread   or the *T* sound

The ancient Egyptians also had a system for writing numbers.

A vertical line = 1
An arched string = 10
A rolled-up string = 100
A lotus flower = 1,000
A finger = 10,000
A god with raised arms = 1,000,000

Here is a counting exercise Sethi had to do: Write the following numbers.

| 34 | 125 | 1,001 | 10,020 |

Home of the High Priest

Sacred Lake

Chapel of Sacred Boats

Holy of Holies

The Great Hypostyle Hall

House of Life

Obelisk

Pylon

Home of the Gods

At the height of its voyage, the sun baked the city of Thebes with its noontime rays. In the House of Life, where the writing lesson continued, it was so hot that the flies didn't even have the strength to fly.

When the teacher saw his pupils yawning, he decided it was time to end the lesson and send them home. Sethi put his writing tools away and rushed out.

After leaving the classroom, he crossed the temple's large inner courtyard and then left through the large front entrance. The temple of the god Amon shimmered in the intense heat. Banners had been raised in front of the temple. In the still air, they hung without moving.

Despite the almost unbearable heat, priests continued about their work in the temple. Each had his own specific task to do. Some had to make sure the god was dressed and fed. Others made sure the fields were properly tilled, and still others wrote the sacred texts that were read during ceremonies.

In the eyes of a child, the temple was the most mysterious and sacred place in the city. Only priests were allowed to enter the private sanctuary where the god was worshiped. Protected from curious onlookers and only accessible to the god's servants, the Holy of Holies was the home of Amon's statue. It was in this chapel that he received offerings of food and drink.

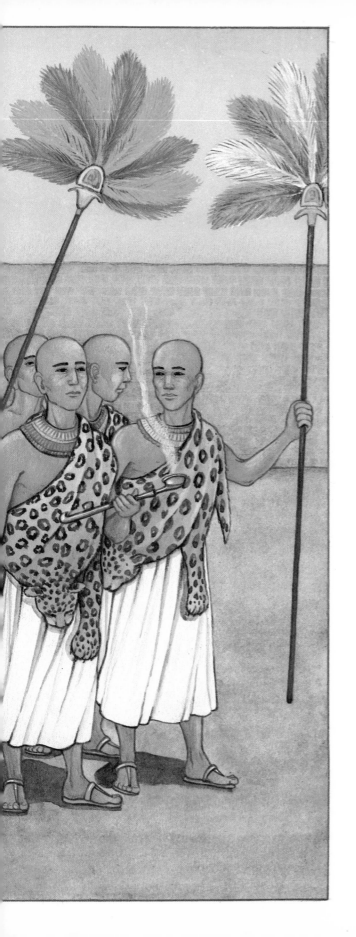

During the great Feast of Opet, Amon and his family left the temple and traveled down the Nile. During this ceremony, which announced the New Year, the priests carried small boats on their shoulders. In them were the images of the divinities.

27

At the head of the procession was the boat carrying Amon. It was made from precious wood and decorated with gold. Next came the boat of his wife, Mut, followed by that of his son, Khonsu.

As the procession went by, the air became filled with the smell of incense. The intoxicating smell came from perfume burners carried by the priests. Some of the priests waved fans and threw sand to purify the ground before the god passed by. Singers sang and musicians played flutes, trumpets, and harps, while the whole city of Thebes followed behind. They joined the procession as it slowly made its way to the banks of the Nile. Faithful worshipers could even approach the boats and ask Amon, the god, questions in front of everyone. Sometimes Amon answered by shaking the boat in which he was seated. It was up to the High Priest to explain what the god's answer meant.

When they reached the Nile, the small boats were placed on much larger ones. These sailed up the river and landed near a temple, where the god was brought. Once a year the priests performed this ritual in the presence of the pharaoh. Later, the procession sailed back down the Nile and returned the god to his usual home.

Sethi sat down under a palm tree and began to think of how wonderful the great Feast of Opet was. Because the teacher had let him out earlier than usual, he decided to enjoy the break and eat the food Madja had prepared for him. There were a few figs, some bread, and a small pastry. After he finished, he headed for the workshops near the temple wall.

Almost every day he stopped at the craftsmen's studio to see his friend Nehri. Nehri was the son of Ipy, a famous craftsman who worked for the temple. The workshop was very noisy when Sethi entered, and he could smell the scents of wood shavings, sawdust, and hot glue. As they worked with their mallets and chisels, the craftsmen discussed the different types of wood they used.

Amon   *Mut*   *Khonsu*

Sethi heard them talk about acacia, tamarisk, jujube, and the wood from different kinds of palm trees. Cedar and ebony were their favorite types of wood, because they were very hard, had a sweet smell, and did not rot. However, those woods were expensive and could only be found in distant lands. Cedar trees grew in the mountains of Phoenicia, and ebony came from the heart of Africa.

"A few years ago," Ipy said, "a big expedition traveled along the coast of the Red Sea in the land of Punt. The travelers were gone several months, and they returned with boats full of myrrh, incense, and sweet-smelling trees, which we replanted."

"That's all they brought back—trees?" Sethi asked.

"Of course not. There were also leopard skins, gold, ivory, and even live monkeys."

Sethi and Nehri were no longer listening to the woodworker. Something was going on in front of the temple. They saw a group of priests rush out of Amon's home. Curious, the two young boys decided to follow them.

The Legend of Osiris

The ancient Egyptians worshiped hundreds of gods and sometimes grouped them together to form a family. Each family was made up of three gods and was called a *triad*. The triad of Thebes included Amon, the father god; Mut, the mother goddess; and Khonsu, the child god.

Osiris, god of the dead; his wife, Isis; and their son, Horus, formed an important triad in Egyptian religion. It was said that when Osiris became king of the world, his brother Set, who was very jealous, wanted to get rid of him. Set built a magnificent coffin, which was just the right size for Osiris, and promised to give it to whoever could fit in it. During a feast, all the guests tried, but only Osiris could lie down in the coffin. Before he could get out, Set slammed the lid shut and threw the coffin into the Nile. Isis recovered her husband's body, but then Set cut it up into small pieces and scattered them all over Egypt to prevent Osiris from coming back to life. Osiris became the symbol of fertile land along the Nile's banks. Set always tries to destroy that symbol by inflicting drought (a lack of water) and famine (a lack of food).

31

The Fertile Land

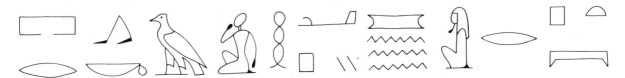

The priests of the temple of Amon hurried toward the river. Sethi and Nehri found it hard to keep up with them. Sometimes the boys even had to push their way through the crowd, which was gathering near the Nile. All of a sudden, they heard loud shouting.

The two children darted in and out of the clusters of curious bystanders. When they reached the river's edge, they came upon one of the most breathtaking sights they had ever seen.

There was a huge boat gliding through the water, heading for the bank where they stood. A countless number of smaller boats pulled the larger boat along while several men, using long oars, guided it in the right direction. Securely attached to the boat's sycamore hull were two pink granite obelisks (four-sided pillars). Cut by slaves in some far-off quarry in the south, these huge stone needles were being brought to Thebes for the temple of Amon.

As the boat was about to come ashore, it swayed to one side. The bystanders watched nervously. A loud creaking noise could be heard as it approached the dock. To everyone's relief the boat steadied itself when lines were tossed ashore and attached to poles along the bank.

33

Workers began to unload the gigantic stone blocks while the priests gave the orders. It was a long and difficult job. Each obelisk was placed on a sledge and held down by ropes. The heavy load was slowly hauled to the temple along a path of wet clay. It helped the sledge to slide along more easily.

Nehri took Sethi by the arm. "Come on, let's not stick around here. We should stay out of the way when they're unloading the obelisks. My father told me that there are often accidents at the docks. It's very dangerous."

Cautiously the two boys left the riverbank. As they turned away, Sethi recognized several workers in the crowd. They normally worked on his father's land.

When the Nile overflowed, the peasants could not till the land because the fields were flooded. During this period they worked building temples. Their job was to cut and transport stones. When the river went back to its normal level, it left behind very fertile black mud called *silt*. The peasants then planted crops like barley, wheat, and flax, which they harvested three months later. There were also beans, lentils, cucumbers, onions, and fruit trees that produced figs, dates, and pomegranates.

Unfortunately the farm laborers' work was sometimes in vain, because field mice, grasshoppers, or sparrows could attack the fields and destroy their crops. When this happened, famine was sure to follow.

Nehri left to return to the workshop, and Sethi continued on alone. As he walked along the bank, he looked at the areas that were still flooded by the Nile. All

of a sudden he froze in his steps. A man had jumped into the water and disturbed a crocodile that had been asleep among the reeds. The monster silently swam toward the swimmer who did not know of the nearby danger. Sethi shouted with all his might. "Watch out! Watch out! Somebody help!"

Alerted by the noise, the man turned around. He saw the crocodile swimming straight at him. The animal's cruel eyes and back scales poked up above the water's surface. It was swimming faster now and had almost reached the man. Thinking this was the end, the swimmer froze with fear and was unable to escape. Luckily, however, some fishermen nearby had already turned their boat around and were heading toward the terrified man. Shouting and waving their arms, the men were able to scare the animal away. It returned to its hiding place, close to the riverbank. There it settled down to wait for its next victim, who might not be so lucky.

The fishermen pulled the tired and frightened swimmer up into the boat. He collapsed among the fishnets that were filled with the day's catch.

"You're the biggest catch we've had today!" one of the men in the boat said to him with a laugh.

From the riverbank, Sethi had seen an unwary swimmer saved. For just a moment he had been scared to death, but now he cheerfully waved goodbye to the fishermen as they moved away on the Nile. The crocodile was considered a sacred animal. But one was better off worshiping it in a temple instead of coming eye to eye with it in the middle of the Nile!

Clay Houses

In Egypt, stones were used only to build temples for the gods or to build tombs for the dead. The homes of mortals—palaces or peasants' homes—were built with clay bricks, wood, or straw. These fragile materials did not resist the passage of time. So today, little remains of ancient Egypt's cities and villages.

To make bricks, Egyptians mixed clay with water and added straw. The mixture was then poured into rectangular molds made of wood. Soft bricks were made, and they were left in the sun to dry. Afterwards they would be used to build houses.

Life, Health, and Prosperity

As he stood in front of his house, Sethi felt the cool evening breeze on his face. For some time now he had been watching the guests arrive for the big banquet his father was giving. Most of them were Rekhmire's old friends from work. Some worked on construction jobs, and others measured the size of his fields after the Nile receded. They did this because many peasants would take advantage of the high waters by moving the markers that showed who was the owner of the field. The peasants tried to increase the size of their fields by stealing land from their neighbors! Each year, Rekhmire had to make sure this did not happen.

Without being seen, Sethi slipped into the room where the meal was being served. His father was seated in the middle of the group on an expensive ebony chair. The chair's legs were carved to look like lions' paws, and ivory had been used for the claws. Rekhmire was wearing a very fine linen garment, a most handsome wig, and a large necklace called a *pectoral*, which was draped over his shoulders. The guests were in groups of two or three. They sat on stools or squatted on the ground.

39

Everyone helped themselves to stuffed goose, roasted chicken, fish, and fruit. The servants made sure that everyone's alabaster cup was filled with wine or beer. All the tables were set with earthenware plates and decorated with lotus flowers.

Sethi's father had forbidden him to mingle with the adults. But the boy was just too curious. He could not resist speaking to Thotmes, Rekhmire's chariot driver.

"Thotmes, I heard that my father went to see Hatshepsut, the queen, today at the big temple."

"Yes, that's right. He was summoned there to measure some of the temple's rooms. He was with Senmut."

"The Minister of Public Works?"

"Yes, he's the one who drew the plans. The queen has reason to be proud. I've never seen such a building before. Everything is perfect in the temple. That's why it's called 'the most wonderful of all wonders.'

"The stones are the most beautiful I've ever seen. Never have there been such skillful sculptors. The artists who painted the walls are the best in all of Egypt. They painted the greatest moments of Hatshepsut's reign. There are paintings of the feast given when she was crowned queen and of all the marvels brought back by boat from the land of Punt. A painter even depicted a giraffe. It's an animal that has never been seen before in Egypt.

"As for Senmut, he had a statue made of himself. He holds the little princess Nefer-neferu-Re in his arms."

Thotmes went on and on talking about Hatshepsut's temple and her reign. He talked for so long that he even forgot to eat! He told Sethi about Egypt's wealth and the peace that reigned on its borders. It had been years since a war had been waged against the people, from the south or the east. Food was plentiful and trade flourished. Egyptian boats sailed the Red Sea and the Mediterranean.

Thotmes said that one day all could disappear and that war and famine could return. But by then Sethi was no longer listening. He was tired from his long day and had fallen asleep on a straw mat on the floor.

Crown of Lower Egypt

Crown of Upper Egypt

Pharaoh wearing the Pschent and carrying the scepters, symbols of his power

The Pharaoh

The Bible referred to the king of Egypt as the *pharaoh*. In Egyptian, *pharaoh* meant "great house" and designated the palace.

The pharaoh was considered to be the son of the supreme god. The golden cobra on the front of his crown and his false beard represented his divine origin.

The pharaoh had many powers. He was the high priest, chief of the army, and the high judge. His authority was symbolized by a crook and a staff, which he held crossed in front of his chest. He also wore a double crown. One was white and represented the south of Egypt (upper). The other was red and represented the north of the country (lower Egypt).

Ramses II on his warrior's chariot

In the Pharaohs' Footsteps

Buildings from ancient Egypt can still be found along the banks of the Nile. Archaeological expeditions have uncovered furniture, jewelry, and sarcophaguses. Today these objects are displayed in a variety of museums. In the United States artifacts from the days of the pharaohs can be found in many museums:

The Santa Barbara Museum of Art, Santa Barbara, California
University of California, Robert H. Lowie Museum of Anthropology,
  Berkeley, California
The Denver Art Museum, Denver, Colorado
Indiana University Museum of Art, Bloomington, Indiana
The Museum of Fine Arts, Boston, Massachusetts
Emory University Museum, Atlanta, Georgia
University of Missouri Museum of Art and Archaeology, Columbia, Missouri
The Brooklyn Museum, Brooklyn, New York
The Metropolitan Museum of Art, New York, New York
University of Pennsylvania, University Museum,
  Philadelphia, Pennsylvania

Children's Games

Egyptian children played with different kinds of toys such as tops, rattles, balls, and dolls.

They also liked games of skill, like fishing or archery. They competed in races and jumping contests. We know all about one of the jumping games from a painting. Two children are seated in front of one another with their arms and legs stretched out almost touching each other. They form a living obstacle that the players must jump over, without falling down.

Queen Hatshepsut

Some Important Dates

Around 3000 B.C.: Narmer is probably the first ruler of Egypt to have unified the North and South of the country into one single kingdom.

Around 2615 to 1991 B.C.: The period of the Old Kingdom. During this period the pyramids were built. The capital was Memphis. The most famous pharaohs were Khufu, Khafre, and Menkaure.

Around 1991 to 1570 B.C.: The period of the Middle Kingdom. Period when the big temples of Thebes, the capital, were built. The most famous rulers were Amenophis, Hatshepsut, Akhenaton, Tutankhamon, and Ramses II.

332 B.C.: Alexander the Great invades Egypt.

30 B.C.: Egypt becomes a Roman province.

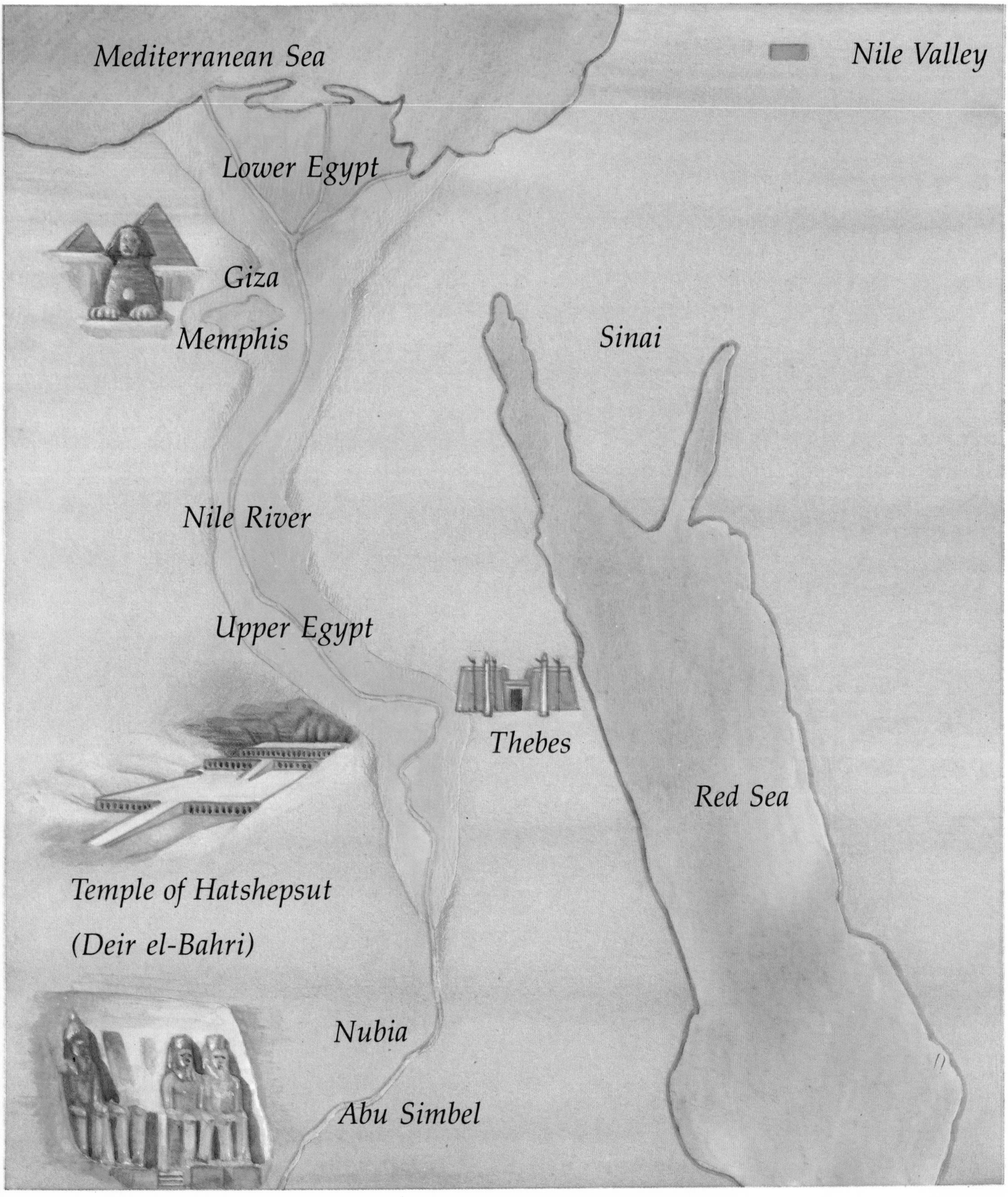

Mediterranean Sea

Nile Valley

Lower Egypt

Giza

Memphis

Sinai

Nile River

Upper Egypt

Thebes

Red Sea

Temple of Hatshepsut
(Deir el-Bahri)

Nubia

Abu Simbel